M. Train

Ray Burton

A Chicago tale

M. Train

Ray Burton
A Chicago tale

ISBN/EAN: 9783337344733

Printed in Europe, USA, Canada, Australia, Japan

Cover: Foto ©Andreas Hilbeck / pixelio.de

More available books at **www.hansebooks.com**

RAY BURTON.

A Chicago Tale.

By, M. TRAIN.

CHICAGO.
1895.

TO MY WIFE.

CHAPTER I.

ON Morgan street, between Monroe and Adams streets, is an old, wooden house, which has for many years enjoyed the distinction of standing almost within the shadows of two well-known public buildings—the Scammon school and the Second Baptist church. The house and my birth-place are identical,—the former an unpretentious residence; the latter a matter of so little consequence that, I have been told on good authority, when I was born the lady next door but one did not hear of it for full ten days after the event, and then only through the loquacity of the milkman; and when she called to see me she gave it as her opinion that Mrs. Burton's boy would be in trousers before the neighbors knew of his arrival.

Births in general are so common and of frequent occurrence that they seldom receive more than a passing notice, and to this one in particular there would attach no interest whatever, were it not for the existence of a tale, which to be told, must be brought from the beginning.

As soon as physical conditions would permit, it was apparent that I had gray eyes—possibly light blue, a very scanty supply of hair which was quite silken, a dimple in my chin, small limbs and hands, and a general diminutive appearance, which was in keeping with the six and one-half pounds which had been entered in my father's memorandum book, together with my sex and the date of my birth. I was a fretful child, I have been told, and the unselfish and loving care shown me by my mother through the first years of my feeble existence is only one example of the same old story, written boldly in the annals of every household, which can be traced out by the seams and wrinkles on every dear, old mother's face. That blessed mother-love that surrounds us in childhood and youth like a halo of glory, is too often allowed to pass without due appreciation, and into the reflections that come with maturer years there steals a rueful poignancy that no amount of repentance can quite remove. Oh restless, impatient childhood! Take time in your youthful days to fall in love with your mother. Make her your sweet-heart, the recip-

ient of your best love and gifts, and in after-
days when, perchance, her face will not be
among those you see daily, the recollection of
having tried to lighten her burdens and brighten
her days will follow you like a benediction.

In writing one's own history, nothing is easier
than hastily passing over that period of childhood in which the memory has received no last-
ing impressions, and about which you know
nothing, only as it has been told you. I shall,
however, recount an incident that occurred in
that uncertain period of my life, the recollection
of which comes to me now like the burden of
some long forgotten song, or what more nearly
expresses it, a dream that I might have had a
month or a year ago. I was playing by the
front door, and by some mishap fell with my
face downward on the step, cutting a gash on
the under part of my chin, and at the same time
biting a hole through my tongue. The screams
that I uttered must have been sufficient to arouse
the whole neighborhood, for the lady next door
but one and my mother arrived on the scene
almost simultaneously, and by their united efforts succeeded in stopping the flow of blood
and soothing the pain. The lady remarked to
mother that the neighbors surely knew of my

existence now, if they had not heard of it before, and accompanied the expression with such
a good-natured laugh, that I thought I might
be persuaded to like her after my tongue and
chin were well. This period between non-rec-
ollection and recollection differs somewhat in
individuals, but I think I must have been at
least three years old when this happened.

About this time I remember of my father
coming home one day and in great excitement
telling mother of a big fire down-town, but that
this part of the city was in no danger. Outside
of our grate I had a very limited idea of
what a fire meant, and consequently was as
ignorant of the magnitude of the conflagration
then in progress and its consequent losses and
sufferings, as if I had been an inhabitant of
some far distant city instead. I recall now that
for many days—even weeks afterward a gloom
seemed to have fallen over our home, and
father talked of "no insurance, total loss, ruin,"
etc., terms that had little meaning to me then.
Those terrible days of destruction, broken for-
tunes and ruined businesses need no recounting
here. That fire stands on the pages of history
without a parallel, and every school boy and
girl is familiar with it.

My father was a partner in a newly organized business venture, and the amount of money found to be his share after that ruthless and premature dissolver of partnerships, was so small that he found it necessary to seek employment in the reconstruction that immediately set in, until his finances would again permit him to engage in business. He was a native of Pennsylvania, his father being of Scotch parentage and his mother of German. My mother was a native of Scotland, emigrating to this country with her parents when but twelve years old. They met in a social way, by attending the same church, and a friendship grew out of the acquaintance which developed into love and marriage. It is not strange that I should feel a kind of proprietorship in the old church, not only because it was the place where my parents met, but because it was the first and only church I had known in early childhood. It is an old landmark of the West Side, standing on the southeast corner of Adams and Sangamon streets, which was, when it was built, in the quietude of a residence district; but now is almost crowded off its own grounds by that ever restless tide of business that each year extends farther and farther outward. It

fronts on Sangamon street, and the patrol box
on the corner stands like a silent sentinel
watching the entrance and warning away any
who might have evil designs upon the building
or the picket fence, that extends the full length
of the Adams street side and on each side of
the doorway. There is nothing about the
structure designed to attract attention, unless it
be its extreme plainness, and that is a result,
most likely, of the strict economy exercised in
its construction, rather than any studied purpose to be plain.

The general appearance within is in keeping
with the exterior,—apparently having been built
to meet a certain want and when that was
reached, it was of little consequence what it
lacked in architectural beauty. At what age I
first accompanied my parents to services in this
church is somewhat obscure in my memory,
but I am sure I had gone there many times before I had been impressed with the sermons.
From my earliest recollection there had always
been the same pastor, the same familiar faces
in the adjacent pews, the same psalm service
and prayer, the same firstly, secondly, etc., in
the sermon, all of which had the humiliating
effect of putting me to sleep, unless I made

strong efforts to resist the drowsy influence,
which I always tried to do, for mother had told
me it was wicked to sleep during services, and
rebuked me severely when I hinted that deacon
W. was a possible sinner. On one particular
Sunday, however, I was all attention, so much
so that father looked significantly to mother
as if to call her attention to the unlooked-for
state of my mind. The regular pastor was not
in his accustomed place, but in his stead a fatherly looking old man, with rather large features,
moderately long hair parted in the middle, and
a plain, conventional coat that insisted on being
buttoned quite up to his chin. At this time I
had been in school a year, perhaps, and had
been taught to read by my mother before I had
attended school, and had read several juvenile
books, among which was a Pilgrim's Progress.
I had formed a very high opinion of the great
dreamer. When we reached home after the
services alluded to, I am sure my parents felt
somewhat disappointed when they found that
my unusual interest on that occasion was not so
much on account of the scholarly discourse as
it was on account of what I insisted was a
marked resemblance between the minister and

the picture of John Bunyan, in my copy of the Pilgrim's Progress.

My having learned to read before I had been to school was partly due to my mother's untiring efforts to instruct me, and partly to a desire she had to keep me out of school until I should attain to what she termed a proper age, although she allowed me to go a term earlier than she first intended, because of my persistent pleading to be permitted to enter, so I could be in the class with my play-fellow, Arthur Gray. Who does not remember his first day at school, and the few weeks following, when everything was so strange, so different from anything he had ever experienced before? For my part those first few days cling to my memory with more tenacity than many of the intervening ones. There was the old school-room with its desks, each one made to accommodate one pupil, and arranged in rows far enough apart to leave the impression that each occupant was expected to attend to his own work; the windows on two sides of the room, with their old-fashioned eight-by-ten panes, the lower ones stained so the inmates could get no glimpse of the outside world; the black-board, that extended across the end and down one side of the room; the teacher's desk, and the large, steel engraving of General Washington that hung on the wall just behind it; the map of the United States on the left wall with each alternate state a different color, giving it the mottled appearance of a crazy quilt; the old eight day clock on the right wall, whose short hand always seemed to move slower as it approached the hours of twelve and four; and of most importance of all, the teacher, a kindly faced woman of rather slight proportions, who, from the happy way she managed every-thing and everybody with whom she had to do, must have had several years of experience in the art of training children. To say that we loved our teacher would hardly express it in sufficiently strong terms. It was a coveted privilege to be permitted to stand by her side, and the little crowd that gathered around her at intermission to show love and to receive notice from her, must have been a source of annoyance; but she never seemed worried with our childish attentions, and usually would take the smallest little girl and the smallest little boy on her lap, and with the larger boys and girls standing around her two and three rows deep, she would tell us little stories, that were quite as interesting as some fables that I had read in a book my father gave me soon after I had learned to read. Arthur occupied a seat just across the aisle from mine, and his little sister, Florence, a pretty black-eyed girl, who had recently been promoted from the primary department, sat in the row beyond him—in the B grade. She was one of those restless little beings who find it next to an impossibility to sit still, which peculiarity often came near getting her into trouble; but Miss Baldwin, our teacher, understanding her temperament, was very lenient toward her.

I found it hard work in this first term at school to keep with my class in everything expected of me, for, as Miss Baldwin said, I was all out of balance. I could read and do some parts of the work quite well, but was woefully lacking in other branches that were of equal importance; so, in order to do the work, I almost always studied at home of evenings, and many times felt discouraged and even wept, when, after having tried harder than ever before on some particular lesson, I found I could not recite as well as some other members of the class who had given it no hard study at all. However, before the year was out and the class promoted, I had evened myself up sufficiently to be able to pass the examination with a record that compared favorably with the rest of my class-mates. As I now look back over that first school year with Miss Baldwin I think the retrospect offords me more pleasure than of any succeeding year that it fell to my lot to attend public school. On being promoted from Miss Baldwin's room we all felt that we were leaving a dear friend, but I took consolation in the fact that she had a few times called at my home, and I was sure she would not discontinue her visits because I was no longer her pupil, and expressed myself to her so, and asked her very cordially to continue to call when convenient, which she assured me she would do, and the mutual friendship that sprang up afterward between her and my mother was largely due, no doubt, to this pressing invitation from an admiring pupil.

My father, by strict economy, had accumulated in a few years after the fire, a moderate sum of money, sufficient to embark in the commission business, having as partner James Wentworth, the style of the firm being Burton & Wentworth. Their place of business was at that geometrically peculiar point just north of

Lake street, where it requires some acquaintance with the locality to determine whether one
is on Market or South Water street, although
the numbers over the doors convey the informa-
tion that the latter terminates at Lake street
and the former begins at the same point. The
front door faced southeast and the rear one
opened on the wharf, where lay the filthy, dis-
colored, inactive water of the river, that bore
on its sluggish bosom no signs as to whether
it belonged to the South, North or Main branch,
and emitting an odor that was offensive even
in a produce market. On this wharf and in the
neighborhood of this rear door lay an unex-
plored region that was very inviting to an eight
year old boy. I was first allowed to view this
forbidden ground from a window, where I
would sit for an hour or more at a time watching the busy river traffic. The shrill whistle of
the tug boat, the deep bass of the steam barge
and the rippling sound of the row·boat as 'it
went sculling by, played a new, wild and fasci-
nating music that was quite captivating to me,
notwithstanding the vile stench that was around
and over all. After I became more accustomed
to the place, father took me to walk on the

wharf and explained many of the objects of interest to be seen there. Just under the abut-ment of the Lake street bridge was a boat builder's shop which was a veritable "Curiosity shop." Near it were old row boats turned up-side down, rusty anchors that looked like they had lain unmolested for ages, old cordage and plunder of one sort and another lying in such profusion, that the approach to the shop, as well as to the flight of steps leading to the bridge above, was almost obstructed. After this inter-esting visit to this busy work-shop, I resolved to see it again—the next time being in the com-pany of Hankins, a man who helped in the store and who had at one time been a sailor. He answered many questions that I asked him about boats and ships, and became quite didac-tic as he noted the interest I took in it. After that I regarded Mr. Hankins as a remarkable man, and held Mr. Cay, the old boat repairer, in about equal esteem, for every time Hankins made a clever point Mr. Cay would say,—"Yes, son, them are facts," and accompanied the ex-pression with a nod that almost dislodged his spectacles, that were hidden away somewhere under his hat. We soon came to be great

friends, and often, on leaving the store after a
Saturday's visit, I would take the back way so
I might look in and shout a parting salutation
to him.

CHAPTER II.

THE outside appearance of our house was very plain and unattractive, so much so that you might pass and repass it daily for years and then not be able to describe any particular thing about its front. It had been painted a dull color because that was conceded to be the best adapted to the smoky atmosphere of the city,—Chicago could not boast of a chartered association for the prevention of the smoke nuisance at that time, else it might have been given a gayer dress. The double front doors opened into a hall, that was in no way different from a dozen other halls in the neighborhood, with two doors, one leading to the parlor, the other to the sitting-room. There was nothing elaborate in the furnishing within, but it made up in neatness what it lacked in ornate qualities, and the well worn armchair and the old fashioned sofa seemed to hold out an invitation to all who entered to recline upon them and rest. From the old piano with its ponderous legs and dark green cover, to the neatly polished kitchen stove there was evidence of good housewifery.

"Ray, have you seen Arthur?"

The person from whom this interrogation came entered the sitting-room from the dining-room, a woman of medium height, gray eyes, dark hair, and perhaps at that time thirty-five years old. She had sad but pleasant features, that wore an expression of solicitude, as if she had it in her mind to ask you if you were quite well, or whether you were not too warm or too cold.

"No, mother, I haven't seen him to-day," I answered, going to her and kissing her, as was my custom when I had been away from the house any length of time.

"He appeared to be very anxious to see you, and said he would come again later."

"Didn't he tell you what he wanted, mother?" said I.

"No, son, but sit by the window, probably you will see him coming soon." I had scarcely seated myself before I saw him coming and I hastened out to meet him.

"Hello, Ray. I have been looking for you all day. I want you to come to my birth-day party tomorrow afternoon," said Arthur. "I will be twelve years old and mother told me I should invite my friends, and of course I want you to be one of the party."

"I can't promise till I ask mother," I replied. "Come and sit in the parlor while I go to see her about it." I soon returned with the intelligence that my mother had given her consent, and when we parted at the gate we were both in a state of high good humor and expectancy.

At the dinner table that evening, after we had finished eating, father remarked,—"Annie, do you remember Mr. Mann, our customer of Champaign, Illinois?"

"Yes, John, the man who sent us the fine strawberries."

"I received a letter from him today," father continued, "in which he tells me of a fine, little farm near town that can be bought for four thousand dollars, cash, which he thinks a bargain. When he was in our store in the spring I expressed a wish to own a farm, which doubtless is the reason he wrote me about this one. I have been thinking seriously about it all day, and believe it worth investigating."

"Perhaps you had better go to see it at once,"

mother replied, "for the trip will do you good even if you fail to make a deal."

After some further talk about the matter, father concluded to go to see the farm, and the following morning took an early leave of us, to be gone two or three days. This new field that had just been opened up to my imagination was almost boundless in resources. I found my mind carrying me on excursions to the fields and wood for wild flowers and berries; I had been to the brook and caught baskets of fish, such, perhaps, as never had been seen in any streamlet in the state; and with my big dog, I had been to the meadows and captured prairie dogs, that had, in reality, retired far beyond the Mississippi river long years ago. Oh, what a wonderful world this would be if the anticipations of youth were ever realized!

So absorbed was I in thoughts of farm life, that, had mother not reminded me, I would have forgotten to prepare for Arthur's party. When ready to go, she called me to her side and said,—"Ray, I am in doubt whether I used good judgment in granting you permission to go to this party. Before very long you will be twelve years old, and by accepting this invitation we make it necessary to give a party to your friends, if we are to keep pace with them. Mr. Gray is an alderman, considered wealthy, and it would be hard for us to give you such an entertainment for your friends as he and Mrs. Gray can give to Arthur and Florence. Society draws lines, my boy, beyond which people of limited means can not go, it matters not how respectable they may be. I am not sure that the Grays have entered that exclusive circle, or whether they are in society at all, but if they should be, it might be better for you to be under no obligations."

"Why, mother, Arthur and I just talk of our sports and have fun together."

"Yes, son, you and Arthur, no doubt, will always be good friends, and perhaps neither will ever be much affected by the set rules of the social world. I wish you a pleasant afternoon, Ray, and now it is time to go."

After a parting kiss I hurried away. My mind was full and I had to check my pace to allow time enough to compose myself. I knew in my heart that one of the anticipated pleasures of the afternoon was to see Florence. I was overflowing, too, with news to tell Arthur about the possibilities of farm life, although I had been told to tell no one about father's business trip. My thoughts would, in spite of me, revert to what mother told me just before I left her side. I could not refrain from an impatient stamp on the walk, when I thought of father as compared with Mr. Gray. I knew he was just as intelligent, and would be just as good an alderman, if he were in the position. (How little I, a boy, knew of an alderman's duties, and what was required to make a successful one.) It seemed to me, too, that mother was better informed, if any difference, than Mrs. Gray appeared to be; and I could not bring myself to look with any allowance upon society, if its mission were to compel the observance of rules that would separate people who were otherwise on visiting terms.

The residence of Mr. George Gray bore a comfortable appearance. There was a liberal stretch of lawn in front and on the east side of the house, and it, like everything else about the premises, was kept in perfect condition. The house was somewhat old-fashioned, with large rooms and wide halls, but splendid looking withal, and doubtless was, when new, one of the best in the neighborhood. It stood on Monroe street near Aberdeen.

As I approached the place I saw Arthur in the front yard, who came to meet me, and, as I was the first arrival, he took me to see his new croquet set. "You see, Ray," he said, "with the new set and the old one, and the swing, we can accommodate about all the boys and girls who will be here."

We chatted incessantly, as we always did when together, and before the others came I had told him a great deal about what might take place sometime, and that, in case it did happen, I was to have a pony and saddle, a dog, and perhaps a gun. Arthur seemed delighted, and said he would come to visit me and we would have a grand time riding on horse-back, hunting and fishing. Just then Mr. Gray came by and stopped to address a few pleasant remarks to us, before passing on to the street. He was a man above medium height, rather portly, with short hair and cropped beard, and a restless eye, that seemed prone to pass rapidly from one object to another in short, erratic glances. The property adjoining belonged to him, and I observed that he walked back and forth on the pavement in front of it, seemingly noticing the effect of a fresh coat of paint that had been given the cornice and casements of the house, with that kind of an admiring look that suggested the rubbing together of hands, which he

was doing industriously all the while. Human
nature was a sealed book to me then, but later
I learned that Mr. Gray belonged to that class
of men, who, when they are pleased with results,
facetiously pat themselves with a good-for-you-
old-boy kind of a pat, that is dearer to them
than caresses from loving hands.

The party passed off pleasantly, and in the
evening, after the boys and girls had gone,
Arthur accompanied me part way home, when
we talked of school, which was soon to reopen.

Early the following evening father returned
from Champaign, and after dinner gave us a
description of his trip. It was at that fruitful
time of the year when mother earth pays and
delivers all that she promised in the flowery
time of May. With orchard boughs bending
with ripening fruit, barns filled with the choic-
est hay and grain, fields of waving corn that
was nearing maturity, and pasture lands teeming
with well-fed stock, what wonder that father
was completely captivated by the scenes; and,
as his thoughts went back to his boyhood days
among the Pennsylvania hills, his heart longed
again for that perfect freedom that can be
found only in the country.

The farm that he had gone to see lay just

without the corporate limits of Champaign, and was perfect in almost every particular. After having told us, in his descriptive way, how he was impressed, he concluded by saying that he had taken preliminary steps toward the purchase of the farm, and if mother were willing he would proceed at once to dispose of his business interests and some vacant lots on Western avenue, which he thought would bring more than the required amount. Mother agreed to the plan, and the days that followed were full of preparations and hope.

CHAPTER III.

IT was in early October when father, having disposed of his business interests and some vacant lots to Mr. Wentworth for a consideration that exceeded, to some extent, the amount needed in the deal, announced his intention of going to Champaign soon to close the trade for the farm. Into the days just preceding this he had crowded more work than was his custom, but never had we seen him more cheerful and happy. In those days I was inflated with a great deal of enthusiasm, and told swelling stories of the kind of pony I expected to have, the carriage we were going to buy, and that I was to enter the university, which is an important feature of that place, as soon as I could pass examination.

On the Saturday before the Monday that father had set for leaving, I accompanied him to Mr. Wentworth's store where he had some unfinished business matters that would require one or two hour's attention, and while he was

thus engaged, I went to visit my old friend, Mr.
Cay. As I drew near his quaint shop I saw,
standing by his side, a boy who delivered papers
in the neighborhood, and who had formerly sold
them near the bridge, where I had first made
his acquaintance more than two years before.
,His name was Frank, which was rather appropriate in his case, for a more honest, open countenance I had never seen among all my associates, and for this reason, doubtless, I became
attached to him. After entering and passing
friendly greetings Mr. Cay said,—"Ray, me
lad, Frank 'as just told me 'ow your father 'as
gone and sold hout to Mr. Wentworth and is
goin' off to the country a farmin'." I replied
that it was so, and entered into a lengthy
description of our arrangements, and had not
exhausted the subject when father looked in
and said he was ready to return home. Mr.
Cay asked him some questions about his change
of business, and while they were talking Frank
said to me,—"You will come down here again
before you leave the city, won't you, Ray?"
" Yes, Frank," I replied, " more than once, perhaps." As we went away, and I recalled the
look that accompanied Frank's question, I
could not suppress the feeling that fate, in some

way, was going to retain us in the city, and
when I thought of all my playfellows and
friends, I almost wished in my heart that it
could be so.

On Monday as we sat at luncheon, father remarked—"General Logan is to address the Grand
Army posts of the city at Central Music Hall
tonight, and I think I can attend the meeting
and then have time to reach the depot for the
eleven o'clock train for Champaign."

"Why, yes, I should think you could, as the
depot is so near there," mother replied.

My father had been in the service during the
civil war, and no one knows better than an old
veteran, how easy it was to shape business so
one could attend a meeting where this loved
comrade and commander was to speak. I had
gone with father to an evening meeting, on Market street near Washington, in the summer, at
which time Generals Logan and Banks, Hons.
S. M. Cullom, Clark E. Carr and Chauncey I.
Filley, were the speakers. I asked him if I
might not go with him to Central Music Hall,
but, as he was not coming home, he thought I
had better not go. Having numerous business
matters to adjust before leaving the city, father
took an early leave of us that afternoon, and as

he boarded an Adams street car, he looked back
to where mother and I were standing and waved
an affectionate farewell.

The next morning as Arthur and I stood at
the corner of Monroe and Morgan streets, where
we usually met before going to school, we saw
Mr. Cay coming toward us from Madison street,
in what seemed an unusually fast pace for him.
When he came up to us he said,—"Ray, is your
father to 'ome?" "No, Mr. Cay," I replied, "he
left the city yesterday to be gone several days."
After a short pause he continued,—"Is the Mis-
ses at 'ome?" I answered mother was at home,
and if he wished to see her I would go with him
to the house, which was near by. After asking
Arthur to wait a few minutes for me, I went
with Mr. Cay to see mother on an errand, the
purport of which I knew nothing and about
which I was beginning to feel inquisitive. On
being shown into the house and introduced, he
refused the offered chair, and said,—"Mrs. Burton, be you sure that Mr. Burton 'as left the
city?"

"It was his purpose to leave last night," said
mother, "but why do you ask, Mr. Cay?"

"The truth his," replied he, "a man was
found in the river near my shop this mornin'

as looked like Mr. Burton, but—." Mother had
fallen to the floor in a swoon. The old man,
after asking me to bring a bowl of water, told
me to bring the nearest physician. I hurried
to do his bidding, but in my bewilderment I
felt like one going about in a dream. I found
Arthur waiting on the corner and told him
mother had fainted and he kindly volunteered
to go for a physician. As I was returning to
the house I looked south and saw Mrs. Wentworth, who had been an intimate friend of my
mother ever since Mr. Wentworth and my
father entered into partnership, coming as fast
as she could walk. When she came up to me,
almost out of breath, I briefly related what had
happened, and she said, kindly putting her
hands on both sides of my face and looking
down into my eyes, while tears were standing
in her own,—"You will have to be a brave little
man now for it is too true, your father is
drowned." She hastened into the house to see
mother, and I sank down upon the steps in a
completely dazed condition. The houses, trees,
church spire and all familiar objects around me
had taken on a strange appearance. Even
Arthur and the physician, who were now ap-
proaching, looked like persons whom I had

never seen. I motioned the doctor toward the door, and, taking Arthur's hands in mine, gave vent to the pent up feelings within me in a storm of sobs and tears. In a short time I was able to tell him what had befallen father. We then went into the house, where we found mother, who had been restored to consciousness, lying on the sofa. Her face was pale and its expression painfully sad; and, in looking back over the years of her widowhood, how well do I know that that look was as abiding with her as if it had been a part of herself, and was the silent exponent of a broken heart.

Mrs. Wentworth, whose home was near us on Sangamon street had been selected to break the sad news to my mother, but Mr. Cay's anxiety had caused him to outrun her in the race to our home, yet the shock to her was no worse, perhaps than it would have been had the intelligence come in a less abrupt manner. In deference to her wish, the funeral was to take place from the house, and the Grand Army post having the matter in charge, arranged to have the remains brought as soon after the inquest as possible.

There were no startling facts brought to light by the coroner and his jury. Only one person

Hulda Jensen, had seen enough to be considered an eye witness; and as the drowning took place between the hours of six and seven o'clock in the evening, the darkness prevented her from seeing very much, and in truth she had been led to make her report to the police more from what she heard than from anything she actually saw. In substance her statement was that she heard a splash in the river, followed by a sound as if someone were struggling in the water, then all was quiet. Immediately after the splash, however, she thought she heard footsteps of persons running north on the wharf. The fact that father had on that afternoon drawn four thousand dollars from the bank, and that all his pockets were turned inside out and everything of value taken, led the jury to come hastily to the conclusion that he had been robbed, and had, while defending himself, either accidentally fallen into the river, or had been thrown in by the robbers, and had come to his death by drowning.

Here was a case for the police to take up and ferret out. Between the hours of six and seven in the evening, when so many people must have been crossing the bridge, why had no one but this one woman heard the splash in the river?

Why had there been no drowning cry from the victim? At this day, no doubt, somewhere filed away among old records that had been in use then, is a description of this case, which has never had written beside it one word that would tend to solve the mystery.

When father's remains were brought home, it seemed to bring mother's sorrow so near to her that it was difficult for her to bear up under it. Never had I witnessed such bitter anguish before; and, out of sympathy, perhaps, more than any realization of my own loss and grief, I wept with her. She was so ill of nervous prostration that it was impossible for her to go to the cemetery. There were no near relatives of either my father or mother residing in the city, but a sister of my father, whom he had not seen since he came west, lived in Pennsylvania, although no one seemed to know exactly where; so, in the funeral procession that followed all that remained of John Burton to its resting place in Rose Hill, that October afternoon, there was but one near of kin—his son; but of kind friends, quite a concourse.

A funeral procession, even to the casual observer, is always a solemn spectacle, but when you are numbered with the mourners, borne slowly on by its measured movement, with ample time for reflection before it arrives at the cemetery, the solemnity becomes almost stifling, and your whole nature asserts a preference for a burial in the wildwood, where formality and crape are not known. ·

It was many days after the burial of my father before mother was strong enough to leave her bed, and much longer still before the physician would permit her to go out of the house. Mrs. Wentworth, Miss Baldwin, Mrs. Gray and many other friends and neighbors called to cheer her and help, if possible, to dispel the gloom that had settled so densely about our fireside; but there was a vacancy that could not be filled, a loneliness and sadness of heart that friendly sympathy could not reach.

There are no words with which to describe the sorrow attending bereavement. It can only be felt, and once deeply felt, its blighting fire, in some cases, burns within the troubled breast throughout life, and, like a daily sacrificial flame, consumes all earthly desires, until, apparently, only the soul remains. Truly, my mother's cup of sorrow was a full measure, but with Christian fortitude she looked to God for strength to sustain her unto the end. And now to my mind there can come no more beautiful thought than that of my mother's simple, unwavering trust in God.

It was on the first Sunday after mother's recovery that the funeral sermon to the memory of my father, was delivered in the church where he had so long been an attendant, and by the minister who was one of his earliest acquaintances and friends in the city. The oration contained no extravagant panegyrics, but dealt with the everyday doings of a busy life that had ever been guided by love and duty, and had, for the good of his family and friends, been cut off many years too soon.

Miss Baldwin accompanied us home from the services and remained that night. Her presence was so consoling and cheering that mother proposed to her to make her home with us, which she accepted on condition that she be allowed to pay the same amount weekly that she paid elsewhere, for board. She belonged to that large army of people, among whom are some of Chicago's most energetic workers, called boarders, and she was not slow to accept a home with a woman for whom she was beginning to feel a sister's love, and between whom and herself there existed such an unrestrained and cordial relationship. Her coming into our home was a blessing in more ways than one, and a home that had suffered such a loss as ours, surely deserved something that could be classed with the good happenings in life. To her I owe what rudimental knowledge I received of the higher common school branches and a few of the sciences. In the years that followed many were the evenings that she willingly postponed any other employment in order to help me over the rough places, in my efforts to master some new subject. This kindness of her was fully appreciated by my mother as well as myself, and we never lost an opportunity to repay her in like deeds.

CHAPTER IV.

MY father died intestate, and, save one vacant lot on which there was a slight incumbrance, he had transferred all his real estate and store belongings, to Mr. Wentworth for a sum of money, almost the entire amount of which he had had with him on that fatal evening of the robbery and his death. Our home, with its old-fashioned furniture, was mother's inheritance from her parents, and of course did not figure in the adjustment of my father's property, it being in her name. If she had possessed any business knowledge or experience she could have settled everything to the satisfaction of all parties interested, at a very small outlay,—and the two or three hundred dollars that must have remained after the funeral expenses were paid, would have been hers to use, at that time when so small a sum would have represented so much to us. On the recommendation of Mr. Gray, however, a young lawyer, Mr. Glynn, was selected to make final settlement of the affairs of the late John Burton; and the greater portion of that remnant of money, that ought to have gone to the widow must have been added to a lawyer's fee for a few hour's work; as there was given to mother, after everything was settled, the small sum of thirty-two dollars. She was not disposed to complain, and it was not until a few years later that she told me the particulars as she remembered them; and, by reference to my father's old account book, I was confronted with the fact that along with the knowledge of my father having been robbed and perhaps murdered by villains, stood the unwelcome revelation that my mother had been robbed, in a small way, by friends. As a boy I had been a close observer of persons, but at this time, which is somewhat in advance of my narrative, I began a careful study of the human animal in all his moods, as I went about my daily duties; and with the passing of the years the interest has in no wise diminished.

It is surprising, too, how much can be learned of the tendencies of human nature, by placing one's conscience as guard over his own actions, and noting the results. For instance, in analyzing the principle that would allow a con-

ductor to pass without paying my fare, which I
had often done without thinking it wrong, I
found that it did not need to be practiced to
any considerable extent until it became a near
relative to the principle that actuates a man in
driving a sharp bargain or permits an adminis-
trator to defraud a widow. Thus, is the human
heart a strange battle ground, on which is waged
an eternal strife for mastery between the good
and the bad, and the result depends largely
upon one's condition, surroundings and am-
bitions.

Mr. Archie Glynn was of a well-to-do family
who resided on Washington boulevard, and
Mr. Gray, in describing the young man's bril-
liant record in college and his bright prospects
as an attorney, could not refrain from touching
on the fact that George Glynn, Esq., his grandfather, had been at one time officially connected with the Bank of England, consequently
there clung to the old English name a hint of
aristocracy, to which he attached a great deal
of importance. This weakness is a matter of
little surprise, however, when we think of the
great number of our countrymen, who, having
reached the very pinnacle of fame and afflu-
ence, travel abroad with their families, and in

many instances marry their daughters to the withered, dwarfed and supernumerary scions of gentility, the latter condescending to tolerate their American alliances for the wealth they bring them, and who in turn are endured on account of the sanguinary blue that courses through their refined beings. Hence, Mr. Gray must not be censured too severely for this peculiarity, for few there be who have not, to some extent at least, this admiration for anything high-sounding.

Whatever may have been the qualifications of young Glynn to entitle him to the confidence of Mr. Gray's friends, certain it was that youth had so lingered in the lap of manhood with him, that it really sounded ridiculous to hear him addressed as mister. In years he was somewhat past his majority, but in looks scarcely eighteen; and each individual hair of his incipient mustache showed that careful training, which was to it what the young man's college training must have been to him—a grand encouragement to future possibilities. He dressed in the very latest style, and his clothes fitted him with such stern exactness that they made him look painfully elegant. I chanced to be at home the last time he came on business connected with the settlement, and among the pleasant remarks addressed to me, while he waited for mother, was this,—"The halcyon days of youth are fraught with more sunshine and gladness than are any others of a whole life-time." The observation would have been more appropriate, perhaps, had it been uttered by an older person, as it seemed to imply that the speaker had himself passed far down the western declivity of life. I did not know that halcyon in any way meant peaceful, nor was I sufficiently posted in logic to be able to draw any comparison between my youthful state and the career of a young kingfisher; and being uncertain of his meaning, I said "Yes, sir," in such an undecided tone that he cast a hasty, half-pitying glance toward me which quite humiliated me.

Although he professed a warm friendship for Miss Baldwin, both being members of the same church, yet he never took occasion to call at our home after that last business visit, and I seldom saw him except when riding his father's spirited horse on the boulevard, which he could perform with the cleverness of a jockey.

CHAPTER V.

THE long, cold winter of 1880–81 had drawn to a close, and the mild spring's sun and shower were wooing back to life the trees, flowers and lawn. It was at this period of my life, when youthful hopes and aspirations ought to have begun to kindle a flame within my bosom tending toward some high destiny, that I was brought face-to-face with a problem, that has confronted many another youth in this great city who was no older nor better equipped to cope with it than was I — the problem of an honest living and how to secure it, independent of charity.

Mother had received a thousand dollars from the insurance company in which father had carried a policy for that amount, soon after his death; but the expenses of the winter had made alarming inroads into it, and I could plainly see that it was a source of much anxiety to her, for I knew it had been her purpose to keep me in school, and now ways and means was a subject that demanded attention and could not be put off longer.

Twice in the winter, after Mr. Woodrow's coal wagon had been to our shed and unloaded coal, had the driver gone away without leaving bills, and as many times had little Grace Wentworth, who was a great favorite in our home, come to visit us and before leaving slipped, each time, a receipted bill into my mother's hand, folded so carefully that Grace was out of hearing before mother knew what the paper was. We tried to accept these tokens of generosity in the spirit that prompted the giver, for it seemed it was more from a kindly feeling Mr. Wentworth had for the family of his old partner and friend than from a disposition to be charitable, and it appeared to be his wish to have us accept it as something he owed us rather than as a gift. We could not, under the circumstances, refuse this kindness, but it made mother feel all the more keenly the need of an income at least equal to our expenses, which in truth was the only thing that would enable her to meet her old friends on equal terms as of former days. I had appealed to her on several occasions to allow me to secure work, which earnings in connection with the amount Miss Baldwin paid weekly, would enable us to meet all bills without drawing further on the insurance money, which could be held in reserve to use in any case of emergency.

One Saturday after we had had a talk on expenses, and mother had partially given her consent for me to secure work after school closed, I walked out upon the street, heedless which way I took and thinking only of the best way to proceed. I seated myself on the steps of the Centenary church and soon was lost to all activity about me, in my mental pictures of myself doing duty in one or another of the various positions suitable to a boy of my age. I had not been sitting very long thus wrapped in my own thoughts until suddenly I felt warm hands pressing my ears and holding my head so I could not turn to see to whom they belonged. Presently a voice as musical as the hands were soft asked me to guess who it was,—an easy task for one who had a boyish admiration for the girl and knew her voice almost as well as that of his mother.

"How could you walk so quietly on these stone steps, Florence?" said I.

"Why, Ray, when you get into one of your thoughtful moods, it would require the tread of

an elephant to attract your attention," she answered, stepping out on the pavement in front
of me, and giving me a mischievous look that
sent little, piercing darts into my already van-
quished heart. I longed for someone with whom
to talk about my plans, and no one would have
pleased me better than Arthur, but out of a false,
foolish pride, I had made up my mind not to
tell him anything about our circumstances; so,
when Florence asked me to play croquet with
them, I excused myself for the time, much
against my wish, promising, however, to call in
the evening for that purpose.

It occurred to me that Mr. Cay might be
able to help me in some way, and acting on the
thought, I went directly home to get permission to go to see him at once, which was
granted, and I hastened away feeling that my
mission was an important one. It was near one
o'clock when I approached the shop, and Mr.
Cay was sitting on his work-bench reading a
paper, and near him lay his little dog, Trip, apparently asleep. Before I was observed, Mr.
Cay laid aside his paper, removed his glasses
and yawned quite audibly, doubtless a preparatory to resuming work. Trip, out of sympathy,
yawned, too, a most lusty yawn and closed his

little, red mouth with a peculiar snap that
seemed to indicate that he, too, had shaken off
the languor of the hour and would look about
him for something useful to do.   His first work
was to discover me just outside the door and to
bark at me in a very threatening manner.   After
seeing that I was an acquaintance, he ran up to
me, displaying all the signs of friendship char-
acteristic of the dog, and in actions if not in
words, bade me welcome.   Mr. Cay greeted me
in his jovial way, and began tying on his shop
apron.   He then partly turned over an old row-
boat that lay against the wall, from underneath
which ran a large, gray rat.   It did not run far,
however, until Trip had it between his jaws
shaking it vigorously.   After killing it he
brought it to his master for approval.   Mr. Cay
stooped down and patted him gently on the
head, and said to me,—"That 'ere may be a rat
with a 'istory.   Many of these large uns 'as
crossed the hocean in wessels."   Then he went
into a lengthy explanation of the habits of the
rat and its disposition to steal on board vessels
and hide in the cargo, and in that way travel
from one continent to another.

It was so interesting to me that I forgot for
a time the business that was uppermost in my

mind and for which I had come to see Mr. Cay. He was then called away from his work for a short time, and, as I sat awaiting his return, I could not suppress a shudder, as the recollection of the mysterious death of my father, which must have taken place very near this shop, came vividly to my mind. It occurred to me, too, as I peered down the dark, zigzag passageway leading to the south side of the bridge, that a more favorable spot could not have been found in the deepest solitudes of a wilderness than was this for the perpetration of a crime. [And at this time, many years since, notwithstanding the bridge turns by electricity and the elevated trains rumble over its upper deck, be it said that beneath is the same dense darkness.] I wondered to myself what could have brought my father to this place that evening, and whether something or some one would ever reveal the facts connected with this tragedy. Just then Mr. Cay returned and I lost no time in telling him of our circumstances and what I wanted to do. He told me very kindly that he knew of nothing that I could do, but that he would see his son-in-law, who was connected with the Western Union service, and probably he would find something for me to do

in their offices. I thanked him and was just
taking leave when a tall, rather portly, light
haired woman hastened by and up the stairway
to the bridge. I observed as she passed that
she looked back, first over one shoulder then
the other, as if to assure herself that no one
was following. I asked Mr. Cay if he knew
her. " No," he said, "but she hoften passes 'ere
and all's seems in a 'urry."

The game of croquet that evening seemed to
lack spirit, and I think it was because I was
withholding my confidence from my best
friend, Arthur.

CHAPTER VI.

THROUGH the kindness of Mr. Cay's son-in-law, William Bright, I was given employment in the central office of the Western Union telegraph company as a messenger. On the first Monday morning in June, the day I was to report for duty, I issued forth, clad in a bright, new regulation uniform, with my lunch box, also of the regulation pattern, to join the great army of bread winners. Everybody was rushing toward the down-town district with all possible haste, prompted, I very soon learned, by the necessity of being on time at their respective places of work. All this was new to me, as I had never before been much on the streets at so early an hour. It appeared to me, as I hurried along Madison street with the throng, that everybody on the West Side had secured jobs the same time I had and were in haste to get to them lest somebody should get there ahead of them. However, I soon became accustomed to the bustle, and up to the present

time I have been mingling with the early morning and late evening crowds, and have noticed
little change in that restless mass of humanity
that moves cityward in the morning and homeward at night, save that each year the throng
becomes a little more dense.

Like myself many people carried lunch, and
the variety of receptacles and manner of carrying them was very amusing to me. There was
the spruce young man, whose box, like mine,
was of the folding kind, who carried it with all
the nonchalance of a lord in the morning, but
who returned in the evening with the box so
snugly hid away in his pocket that no one would
have suspected but that he had dined at Kins-
ley's. The man who hurried around the corner
at Canal and Madison streets, with a russet
hand bag swung over his shoulder by a strap,
might have alighted from the Pennsylvania
limited, but after you had seen him morning
after morning for a few weeks, always carrying
the bag, you concluded that he lived in one of
the suburbs and that the bag contained his
lunch. The girl who carried what seemed to
be a music portfolio in one hand, while with the
other she caught up several inches of superflu-
ous train, was not a member of some early

morning music class, but a cashier in a down-
town store. The food that she could put into
that small box must have been in such Homeo-
pathic particles that it would have made a scant
meal for even a mouse, yet that was her dinner.

When one travels the same street regularly at
a certain hour each day, he soon finds himself
meeting others so repeatedly at the same place
that a kind of tacit acquaintance springs up,
and each looks at the other and smiles, as much
as to say "Good morning Mr. Walker! I see
you are on time," and pass on, neither knowing
anything of the affairs of the other. In my
imagination I often followed those in whom I
became most interested, and pictured to myself
at what and where they might be employed.
The man with the pleasant face and full beard,
whom I met every morning on the Madison
street bridge, I fancied was a ticket agent in the
Union Depot, although he might as well have
been a salesman in a West Side furniture store.
Thus, many things conspired to keep the mind
engaged in those trips to and from work, but
after all they were only the introductory and
finale to a busy matter-of-fact day's duties.

I enjoyed my work very much, principally, I
think, because I realized that I was rendering to

my mother the aid of which she stood so much in need at that time. The first time I met Arthur after I began work was the most trying of all my days in regulation trappings. My pride would not down. I have thought since that it might have been as much on account of Florence as her brother, but at that time I could not bring myself to that acknowledgment. Arthur was very much surprised, to be sure, when he saw me thus attired and with a blushing countenance, but after I had told him everything—that which I had longed to tell him before—he grasped my hand and said I did right in helping my mother, and that I ought not to be ashamed of doing that which seemed my duty. The greatest disappointment to us was the fact that our school days together were ended. I felt relieved of a great burden after having set myself right with him, and I might add that my spirits were further gladdened when Florence said she thought I looked like a young soldier in my uniform. I believed my old friends to be my friends still, and felt that I could face anything in consequence.

How rapidly time flies for those who are constantly employed! The summer had sped by before I could realize that it had more than be-

gun. The games of croquet had been less frequent, it is true, than the summer before, but
this very fact gave us a richer appreciation of
them, and one another, also. The leaves of the
maples began to show a decided tinge of red,
indicating that the genial days of summer were
growing shorter and gradually verging into
autumn,—that delightful yet melancholy season
that arrays itself in bright colors only to re-
mind one that the dress is but a holiday attire
too gay and beautiful to last.

With the coming of autumn came Miss Baldwin, who had been visiting in her native town
in New England, to resume her place in the
public schools. She reminded me that it was
time to lay out a course of study for me to pur-
sue of evenings. Nothing could have pleased
me better. Throughout the following winter
and spring, not only did I keep up the work she
laid out for me, but I found time to practice and
attain a tolerable proficiency in telegraphy. The
boy with whom I practiced this art, I hardly
need say was Arthur. As we were seldom together by day, the hours and half hours two or
three times a week thus spent together of evenings, were regarded as little more than recre-
ation.

CHAPTER VII.

FOUR years have passed since the happenings narrated in the last chapter, and autumn has again appeared in its annual visit, finding me snugly housed in the coop-like office of the Western Union company in the Sherman House. On the particular September afternoon of which I now write, I sat in a half-reflective mood at my post, an open letter before me on the table, so lost to everything about me that my sounder, playing a regular quickstep of "ch" "ch," failed to arouse me. I had been working as an operator for nearly a year, and had been in the office in the Sherman House almost three months. The letter was from Arthur, who had gone to Ann Arbor, Michigan, to arrange to enter the university for the regular course. He wished I could enter with him. How my heart longed to do so, and how keen the disappointment that I could never hope to take a collegiate course! I was brought to myself by a rap on the counter. Looking up I saw a pleasant appearing gentleman who wished to have a message sent, and by the frank he produced I observed that he was a Rock Island official. I immediately sent the telegram, and as he lingered at the counter, apparently in no great hurry, we engaged in conversation. He finally asked me how old I was and how long I had been telegraphing, and added, by way of explanation, that the Rock Island road was extending its lines beyond the Missouri river points, and that many young men, no older than I, were earning from fifty to seventy dollars per month as station agents and operators, and if I should at any time like to try railroad work, he would gladly arrange the matter for me. Before going away he gave me his card, and I thanked him and told him I would take his kind offer under consideration. This was new food for my thoughts. Although Mr. Bright had promised me good pay as soon as I should be able to take charge of a "hot wire," I did not like the prospect of waiting perhaps two or three years before I could hope to reach that proficiency.

Instead of spending the time in study that evening, as was my custom, I went forth to walk and to think,—bending my steps toward

Jefferson park, partly through force of habit, but mostly, I think, because Florence's home lay in that direction. As I was passing Mr. Gray's residence Florence happened to come out on the veranda, and seeing me motioned for me to come in. When I reached the porch she said, "Ray, were you going to pass by and not stop? When Arthur was here you used never to pass by without sounding your special call at least."

"Since he is not at home there probably is no one to answer, or who understands our peculiar whistles," I replied.

"Oh, yes there is. I know every one of them," said she, and at once began to repeat some of them in evidence, until my laughter destroyed the pursed condition of her rose-red lips. After showing her Arthur's letter, she remembered that she had started out to call on a girl friend in the next block, and, as it was in the direction I was going, we walked on together.

We had gone but a short distance, when, before a new residence whose front stood on the modern building line, leaving but a meager strip of lawn in front, Florence stopped suddenly and exclaimed,—"Now, isn't that lovely!" I soon found that the object of her admiration was in the show window,—that recent innovation that finds a place in almost every residence, and puts to very shame the shop windows in the neighborhood. It was not the window itself that attracted her notice, but what she called the exquisite taste in its appointments. Among other things to be seen in that parlor window was a beautiful onyx clock on a brass stand, so arranged as to accommodate the passer-by with the time of day. When I suggested that the clock would look prettier and certainly be more useful if put on the mantel where they could see its face, she replied,—"That's the way with men. They can't see the beautiful in anything."

"Except in women," said I.

She pretended to pout at this rejoinder, but in an instant we were walking on and talking as friendly as ever. As she would be detained but a few minutes at her friend's house, she requested me to wait and we would go homeward together.

Most willingly did I forego a trip to the park for the company of this vivacious creature, who every day appeared to become more charming, and certainly every day seemed to be getting farther and farther away from me and boys of my age. True, I was a few months older than she, but I was a mere stripling while she was developing into young womanhood.

We went home by Adams street, and as we turned into Aberdeen street, we stopped to admire the beautiful grounds of the old Schuttler residence. Before leaving the place I ventured to contrast the old-fashioned places that have ample yard space to the new place before which we had stopped. She said,—"You and Arthur are very much alike in your tastes and are both inclined to old-fogyism."

After parting from Florence at her gate, I walked slowly to my own home in a very unsettled state of mind. It seemed that she was becoming more austere than I thought it possible for her ever to be. A spirit of adventure appeared to have fastened itself upon me, too, that evening, and before I retired I had resolved to persuade mother to allow me to accept a position with the Rock Island company.

CHAPTER VIII.

A LONG blast from the locomotive's whistle announced our approach to a station, and my railway folder of the "Great Albert Lea Route" showed all stations checked as having been passed, on the division on which we were then traveling, up to Horton Junction, into the corporate limits of which place we were now slowly and smoothly gliding. A city? No, but a brisk railroad town which had sprung, as if by magic, (of the mushroom variety,) from a Kansas cornfield.

The Rock Island's lines beyond the Missouri river points were incorporated under the name of the "Chicago Kansas & Nebraska Railroad Co." and continued so for several years, before they were fully adopted and became branches of the mighty parent stem.

At Horton Junction were the extensive shops for these western lines, making it quite an important headquarters. The supply store was here; and it boasted also a fine, new union de-

pot, where arrived and departed no trains but
those of the C. K. & N. road. Here, too, was
a real-estate boom, which, by way of advertis-
ing itself, furnished the electric lights to the
place; and furthermore built a street railway,
that ran about a mile back from the depot, by
the side of certain valuable town lots. It may
truthfully be said that in the two bob-tail cars
on this line no one ever was seen to ride save
the irrepressible small boys. C. K. & N. were
magic letters here, their talismanic influence
permeating the entire municipality. Banks,
newspaper offices and stores regarded them as
better omens of good luck than the well-known
horseshoe. At the hotel I observed that they
had a conspicuous place on the meal tickets,
and even at times, seemed to get mysteriously
mixed up with the hash. They were to be seen
on the caps of all the employes about the
depot and on the trains.

I had just entered the superintendent's office,
on the second floor of the depot building, when
in came a large, dark man, across the front of
whose cap, in white letters, was this word—
"porter", who approached the dignitary of the
room and proceeded to pull off his shoes and to
shine them, while he went on with his pressing

work, a shoeless monarch. [This same superintendent lent a hand in clearing tracks of wrecked cars in the Chicago yards at the time of the great sympathetic railroad strike in 1894.]

He spent one and a half—possibly two minutes of his valuable time looking over my somewhat voluminous letter of recommendation, after which, being once more provided with his footgear, he held a hurried consultation with his clerk, then hastened away to catch a train for Topeka, the Mecca of the system.

The clerk informed me that I was to hold myself in readiness to go out on short notice to do relief work, and as a preparatory step, should spend a short time with trainmaster Bailey, who would catechise me on their order and signal system.

The following winter I spent in Kansas and Nebraska, usually remaining a month at a place, relieving regular agents who wished vacations, and at the end of each month I found myself back at Horton Junction. This unsettled kind of life was not what I was looking for, so I asked for and received a permanent position the following spring, in a town in northwestern Kansas, which for convenience, I shall call Turnerville.

Here, in the springtime, hope rose to its
maximum height in the hearts of the farmers
and stockmen, as they watched with expectant
eyes the growth of the grass and corn. In July
all was changed. What had been a "land of
promise" was converted into a Sahara. The
hot winds had blown over the ill-fated section
and left its inevitable results; and on the farmer's face, where so lately hope had beamed,
now rested a settled look of despair, and on his
farm rested, somewhat less settled, the last
year's mortgage. The suffering that in some
years fell to the lot of man and beast in this
district, on account of drouth, has never been
fully related.

The primitive condition of much of the land
lying adjacent to Turnerville was quite a study
to him who had known of the west only
through reading of it. Here was the sod house,
or "dugout" of the first settler, in a state of de-
cay; the buffalo wallow, now deserted by the
monarch of the plains; the half obliterated
bridle path of the red man; the long-legged,
long-eared jackrabbit; the prowling, cushion-
footed coyote, that deceitful trotter, whose
mangy, dried-up condition Mark Twain aptly
described when he said "a flea would leave it

for a velocipede;" and last, and I might appropriately say, least, the little socialistic prairie dog, whose municipal traits were hardly overdrawn by Irving, in his graphic description of a prairie-dog village. This last named animal afforded me much diversion. In Mr. Turner's pasture, near my station, was a town of them, and I frequently trespassed upon their domains. They were quite shy, and in order to get a view of them at all I had to approach very quietly and then stand motionless for at least a half hour, when, becoming accustomed to my fixed position, one, some distance away, ventured to put his head and shoulders out of his hole and to bark vigorously; then another on the other side of the town became a little braver and showed more of himself and barked in a more threatening manner; then here another and there yet another, until every little mound in the village emitted a protest against the motionless something that had dared to invade their orderly town.

I must confess it made me feel very like a culprit to have all their scolding accusations heaped upon me; so, after I had studied their fussy, chubby figures for a time, I brought my hand up, as in giving the military salute; when lo! the town was deserted and quiet, so suddenly had they disappeared at the first sign of a motion.

I had been at Turnerville four months, when, in July, at the time when the farmer was grieving over his blighted corn, I became similarly depressed by the hand of the company's decapitator. I lost my position by refusing to pay the extra mileage charges that had been assessed on an empty car that had been misrouted from my station. I had sent the car according to telegraphic instructions from the despatcher's office, but had kept no copy of the message, so, when the car accountant traced the matter up, I was left with nothing to show why I had sent the car away from its home lines; and my word, in regard to routing instructions, was not considered. I was constrained to choose between paying the mileage and losing my position, and I chose the latter.

When the villagers heard that I was to leave, they wrote up and signed, without my knowledge, a petition to the general manager at Topeka, praying him to have me reinstated. They told me what they had done and gave me a duplicate of the papers. I thanked them heartily for their expressed interest in me, but told them it would have no weight with railroad officials. Ever since then I have had a tender regard for those honest folks of Turnerville.

After this misfortune there seemed to be nothing for me to do but to return to Chicago, which I did very soon, and where I have since resided.

CHAPTER IX.

I HAD been gone less than a year, and it was not without some sense of chagrin that I returned so soon, but when I observed my mother's joy at having me with her, the vexations of my railroad experience were soon forgotten.

In so short a time little changes had taken place which were apparent to me, that no doubt escaped the notice of others. My mother, whose health was never fully restored after the shock received at the death of my father, was noticeably thinner and paler. The silver in Miss Baldwin's hair showed very much plainer than when I left,—in fact I do not think I had ever noticed it before. Grace Wentworth, whom I had always regarded as a little sister, I was astonished to find had grown too large to be kissed by me and had assumed coy and ladylike manners. She had made remarkable progress in music in the past year, being almost a musical prodigy,—according to her teacher's way of stating it. Mother remarked, casually

that she thought Grace was becoming hand-
some. No one who knew her doubted it, but
one had to be acquainted with her to observe
the fact. Florence was as jolly as ever, but the
ring of her laughter showed traces of education,
and she assumed an unnatural manner of walking. But one must consider that the hearty
laugh, and merry skip of childhood cannot
always remain with us. Arthur was home on
vacation. In him there was little change, being the same dear friend he always had been.

On the whole, I felt glad to be at home again
and to live within its influence. But I could
not long remain idle, I must seek employment.
Did you ever seek employment? You found
her a coy creature, I dare say!

I would go to see Mr. Bright, in the Western
Union office.

On my way there my footsteps seemed naturally to take the direction of the old boat shop.
I am unable to explain just why it attracted me.
It was anything but an attractive place. It may
have been on account of my early associations
with the locality, but most likely because of
the kind hearted, fatherly Mr. Cay, who was
always to be found busy at work in this shop.

How narrow the river seemed, now that I had

seen the Father of Waters! Even at the fork
north of the Lake street bridge it illy deserved
the name of river, as to width, and as to cur-
rent, never.

If there was any change on the wharf near
the shop it was probably that a few more rusty
anchors had been added to the old time number, that had lain there since my first knowledge of the place.

Mr. Cay and Trip observed me at the same
time and both came forward to greet me.

"'Ello, Ray, me boy, 'ow-do-you-do!"

I shook the old man's hand with as much
eagerness as I could have shown for a near relative.

Trip held up his paw to be "shook," a trick
that I had taught him, and further expressed
his delight by wagging his tail in such a rapid
succession of raps against the leg of the work-
bench, that I was fearful lest he should injure
that restless appendage.

In the chat that ensued I learned that Mr.
Bright had been transferred to Denver, on account of his health; the woman never passed
that way any more; and Frank was delivering
papers over a West Side route. Mr. Cay suggested that I should go the Western Union com-

pany again. He thought it likely that they would give me my old place. I told him that I had set out to do that very thing,—and was just going, when he said,—

"Ray, do you remember 'Ankins?"

"Hankins, the man who once worked in the store?" I asked.

"Yes."

"Oh, yes, I recollect somewhat of him! What about him, Mr. Cay?"

"He was 'ere the hother day, and was hasking about you. He is sailing on the lakes now-a-days."

"I remember he was a sailor. Good-by, Mr. Cay!"

"Good-day, me boy!"

I left my application with the telegraph company that day, but was told that they were not in need of help at the time. That done, I began a careful search through the "want" columns of the dailies.

This means of procuring employment partakes somewhat of the nature of a game of chance, or lottery. Certainly the number of letters one writes in answer to advertisements before receiving a reply, corresponds very nearly to the usual number of blanks to a

prize. The possibilities that one's mind con-
jures up and dwells upon, while waiting for
these answers that never come, serve to keep
one's courage up to the sticking point. One
feels equal to anything,—in fact able to cope
with a high salaried bank position, but is not
surprised, when, later on, he accepts a position
as general utility man in a department store.

In a few weeks, after having exhausted my
entire stock of epistolary lore, as well as my
stationery, I secured a position as entry clerk
in a wholesale clothing house. This firm, E. L.
Warp & Co., did a thriving business in Monroe
street, not far distant from the river.

The experience I had received at way-billing
and checking way-bills, enabled me to take up
the work of entering, extending and billing
without any trouble.

"Why did you take a place in a clothing
store, Ray?" Arthur asked, when I told him of
my work.

"Because it was necessary for me to be employed, and this was the first thing that offered."

"If you had waited a little longer probably
you could have secured a position at telegraphing."

"If I liked that kind of work as well as you do, Arthur, I, no doubt, would have had the patience to have waited indefinitely; but the truth is, I rather wished for something different."

Arthur was such an enthusiast on electricity, especially as applied to telegraphy, that he had a battery and instrument in his room at school, and had earned the name of electrician from his associates.

CHAPTER X.

THE shipping room of E. L. Warp & Co.'s
establishment was not very different, in
most particulars, from other shipping rooms in
the neighborhood. My desk, although inclined
to be migratory in its habits, was considered a
near neighbor to the shipping clerk's desk;
and, on account of their common interests,
(and I might consistently add, aspects,) the
one was very often mistaken for the other.
Likewise their respective clerks.

After one has worked at a certain desk for a
considerable time he comes to regard the various objects on and about it as old acquaintances, and is on good terms or quarrels with
them in the proportion that they are in or out
of their proper places.

On the end of the desk hung my memorandum hook, which had the capacity for an un-
limited amount of chaotic matter, consisting of
sundry overcharges, undercharges, corrected
terms, etc. One needed the patience of Job to

reduce it to anything like order. It never had been entirely cleared of its accumulation of papers; probably because, like the wonderful pitcher of Mother Baucis, it was played upon by some occult means of supply.

By the shipping clerk's desk hung the Shipper's Guide. It was an universal friend. With its peculiar binding, the square, black advertisement of the Burlington Route on the front cover, its white, green and yellow leaves, very much besmeared with ink, it impressed its identity so firmly upon one's mind that he had but to think of it to see it.

Suspended from the ceiling near the center of the room hung an immense arc light, which with all the care bestowed by a kindly disposed electrician, had a habit of "flickering," often at the very time when most needed. In this particular, I now remember, it was not very different from certain animate objects that held positions in the same house with it.

The shipping clerk, Tom Bluford, was among the first with whom I became intimate. He was a sort of all-around genius but was exceptionally apt with the marking brush, which he wielded with all the dexterity of Freytag's Herr Pix. He had reached middle life, was a kind-hearted man and very much liked by his employers and associates.

Charles Snyder, whose grandfather probably wrote his name Schneider, was order clerk, who attended to charging the goods. He and I were thrown together very much in our work. Henry Grubb, who helped Charles and who followed him like his shadow, was often jokingly called "Friday."

In the extreme end of the basement near the boilers with scarcely a ray of daylight falling upon it, stood the desk of Herman Pfoutz, the engineer. He had spent his boyhood days on his grandfather's Wisconsin farm, where he had learned to love both the song and the freedom of the robin; yet we find him engaged in a life's work that isolated him from nature's rural voluptuousness.

It occurred to me that certainly in this and like places the employe spends the daytime of his life in a dungeon, from which he emerges at night to mingle with the people of the outside world. It may be that he is the respected head of a family, and is looked up to with love and pride. He may be "a man among men" in his lodge, town or social meetings. It is possible that he and his good wife occupy reserved seats in the front row at the church or theatre. When morning comes, however, he hastens away, not so much from eagerness as from habit, to again entomb himself, as in a cloister, for the space of another day. He left his home in the morning, a man; he entered upon his duties, a machine. Smooth-running it may be, yet a machine.

I, too, became a machine of this sort.

The concern of E. L. Warp & Co. might be compared to a piece of complex machinery, the mainspring of which was Mr. Hildebrand, the manager. He was a small man, pleasant but alert. He had a way of smiling clear through you, (if you will allow the expression,) without disturbing your anatomcial construction. Method was everything with him. His initial, as signature on orders, was always placed in a certain position, and looked as much like any one of the other twenty-five letters as it did like the letter H that it was intended to represent. This enigmatical manner of signing is rather a common peculiarity, I believe, in business circles, and, like smoking or wearing creases in the trousers, bespeaks a certain degree of style. However, he could write a good business hand when it was his pleasure.

When standing at the desk referring to ledger entries, one was liable to mistake him for the office boy, but when he turned up pages and jotted down data in true Tim Linkinwater accuracy and rapidity, one somehow agreed with the office girls, that he was a remarkable man.

CHAPTER XI.

AFTER I had been six months or more with E. L. Warp & Co., I learned incidentally that the shipping clerk was soon to be allowed an assistant. I lost no time in seeing Mr. Bluford about the place for my newsboy friend, Frank. His application was considered and he was given the position. I was glad to be of assistance to him, for I knew him to be a worthy, industrious boy; and I had heard Mr. Cay say that he had a widowed mother whom he helped to a living, although he seldom spoke of her himself.

Frank was a strong, well developed boy and soon made himself so useful that he was thought to be indispensable, and was kept, not only through the busy season, but all the year round.

There was one other employe of whom I wish to speak before passing this point, a sort of petty manager, of the name of Loftie. He prided himself on the fact that he had been born New York city, and was so enthusiastic over anything that bore any reference to Gotham, that, it was averred by some of the boys, he actually doffed his hat on meeting a Knickerbocker ice wagon.

Mr. Loftie would have had more friends among us had he not on all occasions disseminated such an extravagant air of superiority. In conversation he was quite a sputterer, and left one with a sort of confused impression of whiskers and verbosity, and one could hardly determine which was the more crinkled and twisted.

To hear him job off a lot of odds and ends to a Clark street dealer, led one to conclude that, after all, he was an important man in a small way.

His introduction to the shipping room, soon after he came to the house, was rather cyclonic in its main features. He came rushing in and exploded in our midst,—these words flying haphazard like so many shot from a canister:

"I say, Mr. Bluford, what's in this bale, and by what road did it come? I want to keep tab on these things, don't you know!"

"The bale was routed over the 'Hair line, and contains a piece of 'airline cloth," Mr. Bluford made answer; and each stared at the other as much as to say,—"I like your style."

The shipping room was a general resort at noon for almost all the men and boys who brought luncheon with them. Henry Grubb was always ready with a discourse on the delicacies that his wife had just made from certain products that he had procured the day before on South Water street, thus making our mouths water, and unintentionally aiding us in the mastication of our dry food.

Charles Snyder's talk when not of an epicurean nature, turned to gunning and fishing. He had gone with certain members of the firm, before their business had assumed very considerable proportions, on camping expeditions to Wisconsin, where they had fished from the same boat, slept in the same tent and probably drunk from the same decanter. He told many interesting incidents of these outings, and retold many of them each season with clocklike regularity. They were very diverting to the newcomers.

And the old packer, who had sailed before the mast, and also spent some years in the gold fields of Australia, never lacked an audience when he felt disposed to talk.

Then, too, there was the quiet man, who was
an all-around assistant. He had not much to
say of exploits abroad, but was full of informa-
tion on general topics.   At the time of the civil
war, he was a lad working on an Indiana farm,
when his elder brothers, with thousands of other
young men, donned the blue uniform, shoul-
dered the musket and marched away to the
front.   In the last call for volunteers, he himself, had gone, young as he was, but "Appo-
mattox" had been freshly inscribed on history's
pages ere they had passed the limits of their
own state.

He had been, all through his life, a close observer, and a real student of Nature. He understood the habits of animals, and knew all the
wild flowers of this latitude and was able to give
the medicinal properties of the more important
ones.   The names of trees and shrubs he told
off like reciting a well learned lesson.

We had walked one afternoon in the groves
bordering on the Desplaines river, far away from
the city's bustle, where Nature articulates a lan-
guage peculiarly her own and far too plain to
be misunderstood by her votaries. I here learned
that he was a Thoreau woodman. (The reader
will excuse what appears to be a pun at the ex-

pense of one of the most unique of American naturalists, when I explain that I mean he was much like that eminent woodman in his careful observation.) When in the woods he was altogether a changed man. He seemed to commune with the trees and shrubs about him as they appeared to reach out their graceful braches to welcome him. He pointed out trees that were near of kin, so to speak, and explained the characteristics by which this relationship was known. The same he did with the flowers. This was the most profitable ramble I had ever taken in the woodland.

It was my good fortune to spend a half day with this quiet man in Jackson park in the summer of 1893. I had not seen him before that time for several years, nor do I now know his whereabouts. Of course we visited the forestry building, because it was where his inclinations led him, and I was glad of the opportunity of so learned a guide. When we approached Indiana's exhibit, he said:

"Young man, I'll wager a double round at the White Horse," (which was not much when one recalls the construction of the mugs,) "that I can name any or all of the trees in the collection."

Without accepting the bet, I put him to the test and found him equal to the task.

But I have digressed. To return to the shipping room, it was this quiet man who amused us younger people most of all with stories of his boyhood. Fishing for bass was one of his favorite sports. No lessons in theoretic casting had he ever taken. He laughed at the idea. He told of the wood-pheasant and how it did its drumming; of the opossum and its peculiar manner of carrying its young, and that its nearest kinsman lives in far away Australia; and of the otter and its style of coasting without the aid of snow. He had found many Indian relics, and had played by the grave of Peter Cornstalk, an Indian chief, who is buried on a hill-side by Pete's Run, a small stream that perpetuates his name.

Thus, were our noonings spent in pleasant chat, and especially interesting they were for the few months that the quiet man was with us.

CHAPTER XII.

WORKING day by day with Frank enabled me to observe that there was nothing coarse about his personal appearance or actions, such as one might naturally expect to see in a boy brought up in the street. He possessed an attractive face. There played within his laughing eyes a peculiar twinkle that reminded me of someone else whom I frequently met. It was several days, however, before I found out which of my acquaintances bore the resemblance, and many more before I made an interesting discovery, that will have some bearing on this tale, as developments will show.

Frank had spoken several times about having gone on errands to a certain physician's, which aroused my curiosity and on inquiry I found that his mother had been suffering of lung trouble, and that he had received encouraging words from the doctor. I was pleased to know that he took so much interest in his mother's welfare, but I could not keep my mind from dwelling on the fact that the physician to whom his mother had sent him was none other than our old family doctor who had lately established himself in a downtown office for certain hours of each day.

It was about this time that I became fully aware of the material growth of our old neighbors—the Grays. They had shown symptoms of opulence in many little apparently accidental ways, which, on close investigation, proved to be a sort of hand-bill advertisement of the fact.

Florence had once told me in a burst of confidence, that her father could make a thousand dollars or more almost with one stroke of his pen; and that, with her limited knowledge of the shrewd diplomacy of her aldermanic father, was a mere shadow of the real earnings of this great municipal legislator.

Some years before I had heard Mr. Gray remark to some gentlemen, who, Arthur had told me, were promoters of a great improvement corporation—whatever that meant—that he would fix that little matter at the next meeting. He had now been in his ward's service for six years, and, after Florence's confidence, I could not help recalling her father's words, and wondered to myself how many, many times he must have "fixed matters" during his long term in office.

At that time as well as now, there was sandbagging in dark alleys by footpads, and there was sandbagging in legislative and commercial halls by the very pillars of our social system. Here, in this city, on whose soil not many decades ago roamed the unlettered savage, (subsisting on wild game, seasoned to some extent no doubt with the aromatic vegetable after which it was named,) there has risen a modern savage, whose perfidy transcends that of his dusky brother of half a century ago. The erstwhile savage wore beads,—the present specimen wears diamonds.

The study of civilization has so many standpoints from which it may be scrutinized, that it becomes a difficult matter to say with any degree of certainty that such-and-such were barbarous ages or that some other is the exemplification of civilized refinement.

At the last election, however, Mr. Gray failed of reelection, and, as if to punish his old constituents for derelict duties, he had shortly thereafter removed from the ward to a palatial residence on Washington boulevard near Garfieid park. The acquisition of this valuable property was what led me to conclude that they were really accumulating wealth.

I passed by their old home on Monroe street a few days after their departure. It was tenanted by strangers, and in the front window hung a card bearing this legend—"Rooms to Rent."

It was not without a feeling of sadness that I looked upon these changes and thought of the childhood joys that positively had terminated with them.

CHAPTER XIII.

ONE evening as I returned rather belated from an errand to the North Side, I stopped by the "Bx" Western Union office, in Wabash avenue near Lake street, to watch an operator in his rush of eastern work as he sat at the New York table. As I stood partly hidden in the alley, looking through the window at this agile manipulator of Morse, my thoughts went back to the time when I was similarly employed, and when a very good friend of mine occupied a position in this same office.

How long I stood thus absorbed I can not now recall, but I remember that I became conscious that some one was near me. I peered cautiously over my shoulder and beheld Mr. Wentworth on the sidewalk on the opposite side of the alley with his back toward me, talking in a low tone to the very woman whom I had seen near Mr. Cay's shop. Evidently I had not been seen by Mr. Wentworth. I could account for his being in this locality, as he had

but recently traded his commission store for a
business in River street. I did not want to reveal myself nor did I wish to eavesdrop. I
was an unwilling listener, but the only words
that I heard distinctly were these from the
woman—"Your sin is greater than mine." Mr.
Wentworth placed what seemed to be money
in her hand, and they separated, he going south
and she north.

An irresistible impulse took possession of me
to follow this woman. Shadowing was a new
role to me, and under any other circumstances
would have been abandoned. She turned west
into South Water street and it being very dark
I almost lost trace of her. At Dearborn street
she bent her steps southward and paused directly under the lamp by the Commercial hotel,
apparently undecided which way to go. I came
up and walked on to the opposite corner. I
observed in passing that she was older than she
appeared to be, seen at some distance, and that
her face wore that ghastly look that unerringly
marks the consumptive. Her halt was short.
She went west in Lake street at a rapid pace,
and I, on the opposite side kept a short distance behind. She crossed the street at Market and passed quickly over the bridge on the

south walk, turned north into Clinton street and
passed up a stairway on the east side almost
opposite the Chicago shot works. This probably was the abode of this mysterious woman.

I took a survey of this triangular block,
whose longest angle projects northward like
the prow of some cumbersome freight vessel,
and was convinced that it was the haunts of all
sorts of wicked characters. I could not class
this woman with such. However I had nothing
but looks from which to judge. The little
business rooms that might be compared to its
forecastle, were occupied by a lager beer ven-
der, on whose windows was displayed this
somewhat biblical inscription—"The House of
David." The struggling gaslight could hardly
penetrate the smoky darkness, and the sub-
dued moonlight rather imperfectly revealed the
top of the majestic shot tower which seemed to
enjoy existence in an altogether different atmosphere from this smoke-begrimed street.
Everything was repulsive. Even the very mud
in the gutter appeared to hold itself up as a
sample of the filthiest of its kind.

With every step that I placed between myself and this questionable locality came a feeling of relief as if awaking from a nightmare.

I was none the wiser for having followed this
woman, and felt heartily ashamed of the act.
As I walked homeward, however, these words
kept ringing in my ears—"Your sin is greater
than mine."   I did not understand them, but I
resolved to tell no one, and await developments.

CHAPTER XIV.

A FEW weeks later, Frank failed to put in an appearance one morning, and later in the day sent word that his mother was very sick. That evening on leaving the store I secured his number from the usher, for the purpose of looking them up. I was greatly surprised when I again found myself in Clinton street and near the shot tower. Excited curiosity was fast taking the place of friendly interest, by this time. Sure enough, there was the identical stairway up the flight of which I had seen the mysterious woman pass. I paused a short time at the foot to compose myself, and then quietly proceeded to the rooms above, where I saw on a poor but clean bed in the farther room, the wasted form of the woman whom I had but recently shadowed. Frank met me with a kind but sad smile. His mother looked at me rather blankly for an instant, and then, seeming to recognize me, motioned me to a seat near her, and bade Frank go on an errand to the druggist's.

"Mr. Burton," she remarked, after Frank had gone, "I have wanted an opportunity to thank you for your kindness to my boy. You look surprised, and well you may. Talking is difficult. Ah, me!" After lying motionless with her eyes closed for a short time, apparently collecting her thoughts, she resumed: "How much you resemble your father! You see, I have known you a long time. When you were just a little baby, I lived with my mother next door but one to your folks, on Morgan street. Then I was a proud young woman with bright prospects. By placing too much confidence in the promises of a certain man, all was changed. Humiliation killed my poor mother. You surely will keep this secret from a dying woman. I feel that I can trust you. Mr. Wentworth, your father's old partner, is Frank's father, but the boy does not know it. That is not all,—" Here she was overcome by a fit of coughing, and when she had recovered sufficiently to again talk, Frank had returned. I gave them such words of sympathy as my puzzled brain would permit at that time, and after assuring them that I would call again soon, I withdrew.

I took a circuitous way home, so I should have ample time to think about these disclosures. I now understood the words—"Your sin is greater than mine." How strange it all seemed to me! Grace Wentworth was the one who bore some resemblance to Frank, who was, innocently enough to be sure, so nearly related to her.

My brain refused sleep that night; and, in the still watches, when I was sorely perplexed about this secret that had been intrusted to my keeping, that poor, outraged life in the rooms in Clinton street, went out. I never heard from her lips what more she had to reveal. Hulda Jansen was dead, and I kept her secret a long time thereafter.

CHAPTER XV.

ONE Sunday, several months after the Grays had left our neighborhood, I went to Lincoln park to visit "my pets," as I was wont to style the animals. I never tired of watching the pelican and his wife on a fishing voyage. They are the real fishers of nature, being provided with a sort of dipnet appendage, through the meshes of which no fish ever escapes. When one made a sweep with this extended pouch, the other did likewise and in the same direction, giving to their concerted action rather an automatic appearance. When one caught a fish he held his head up and began such a shaking of that capacious trap and snapping of those long mandibles, as to create quite a commotion in the water and to bring further proceedings to a standstill. This was done presumably to kill the fish, or at least to deprive it of a portion of its wriggling power, before swallowing it.

The somewhat circumscribed prairie-dog

village is another interesting spot, but its little, saucy denizens are as different from their wild kind as are the urban newsboys from their country cousins.

On this particular visit I lingered by the bear dens longer than at any other place. I observed that the polar bear, in his monotonous, semicircular motion, appeared to place his feet, at each repeated swing, in his former tracks, which seemed to have worn depressions in the cement and stones. Among the black bears was one uglier than the rest, that betrayed the faculty of appreciating applause. It performed many cunning tricks to the constant delight of the on-lookers. Among other pranks it actually tried to embrace a stream of water that the keeper saw fit to turn upon it.

As I turned away from these diverting scenes, whom should I meet face to face but Florence Gray escorted by Mr. Archie Glynn. That Mr. Glynn should not remember me was no surprise, but to be looked at blankly and passed by unrecognized by an old acquaintance and schoolmate, was more than I could endure. I seated myself on a bench near by and took up a train of thoughts that may have lasted for hours for all I now remember of the lapse of time.   It marked a turning point in my life.

I then and there resolved to take up the study of stenography.   I realized fully that the girl for whom I had cared, in a shy sort of way, for so long a time had out-grown me to the extent that she associated with a man who was ten years my senior, and was ashamed to recognize me in his presence.   I felt that I could do nothing to bring my maturity up to her ideal, therefore, with a feeling of discontent, born of a desire to rise, I took this method of bettering my condition, not, however, with a hope of ever attracting Florence Gray's attention again.

To any one who has gone through the task of learning the multiplicity of meaning to be had from a few deflected, inflected, curved, vertical and horizontal lines, punctuated, as it were, with a sprinkling of dots and dashes, an explanation of the hard work that I encountered is unnecessary.

During the winter following this resolution I made rapid progress in shorthand by working at night.   When spring came, many a Sunday morning found me, with other would-be report_ers, seated high up in a certain religious sanctuary, endeavoring to "take down" the deliberately enunciated sermon. I found this to be excellent practice, however much it appeared to divert the gospel truths from their wonted channel.

I can say truthfully, as a sort of apology to my conscience on this score, that many times after those days of practice, did I resort to that same sanctuary, attracted thither by the logical as well as the ethical purity of the sermons.

Early in the following summer I went to Valparaiso, Indiana, where I spent a term in the Northern Indiana Normal School, devoting all my time to speed exercises in shorthand. I went there on the recommendation of a friend, not because I could not have had the same training here, but because I wished to get away from the city, where there would be nothing to attract me from the subject in hand. There I made rapid advancement, and quit the place with feelings of regret, because of the warm friends among the teachers and students whom I should most likely never see again. This oft repeated aphorism of one of the professors was like an inspiration to me—"You will be successful in your work just to the extent that your honest efforts merit success." These remarks were directed more particularly to those students who were preparing to become teachers in the public schools, but appropriately applied to any of us.

Hundreds of boys and girls of limited means have gone there and received such instruction as enabled them to help themselves, who probably never could have gone beyond the district schools, had it not been for the low tuition and cheap board offered at this institute. Few indeed there were, who, after having spent some time in this workshop, left without taking with them some of the magnetic sparks of enthusiasm that permeate the atmosphere of the school.

CHAPTER XVI.

I WAS very agreeably surprised on my return from Valparaiso, to learn that Mr. Wentworth had arranged with Judge L—, with whom he was intimately acquainted, to give me a trial at court reporting. I went to work at once and soon became accustomed to the routine. I found it more to my liking than anything I had yet done.

Mr. Wentworth, who now owned a snug home on Jackson boulevard, had but recently purchased a new surrey, and nothing seemed to please him better than to drive by and take mother, or some one of our family with them when they went driving. He appeared in his best mood, however, when only Grace and myself were with him. He, at such times, insisted that we should occupy the rear seat while he sat before and attended to the driving. Grace and I pretended that we were wealthy folks and that Mr. Wentworth was our coachman. In all of our jokes and fun he took as much interest as though he were a boy. He said it made him feel young to be with such chickens as we were.

When I called at their house, he invariably took us off to the parlor where he would turn the music while Grace played her latest pieces. Often he said,—"Now Grace play just one more for Ray before he goes"—always leaving the impression that it was expressly for me.

Mother, Miss Baldwin and I had many rides that summer and fall, all because of Mr. Wentworth's new carraige. I was pleased most of all on mother's account; as she was in poor health and it seemed to do her so much good to get out. Late in the fall she had gone with them to Jackson park, and thus got to see the World's Fair buildings, then nearing completion, although the fair itself she was not permitted to see.

One day when we were remarking about Mr. Wentworth's attentions to us of late, Miss Baldwin said,—"I think, Ray, that Mr. Wentworth's intentions are to have you and Grace marry, providing he can have his way about it."

"Why, Miss Baldwin, what a fertile imagination you have!"

"I imagine nothing, Ray, but I have observed many actions that have to me but one meaning. I should be very much pleased myself, because I always wish the best for you, and I think Grace a jewel."

There can be no doubt but at that time I felt growing upon me a fondness for Grace's society. It came unsolicited. We enjoyed being together because we were untrammeled by any stiff rules, and felt at liberty to talk and act almost with the freedom of a brother and sister. I am quite sure Grace regarded me in no other light than that of a brother. Her refined sensibilities would have received a severe shock had she suspected that which Miss Baldwin's penetration fathomed. It would have appeared to her like trafficking in futures with human souls as a commodity.

I knew enough of Grace to know that if I *should* awaken to the realization that I loved her, I would have to woo and win her. She was not of that disposition to be just simply given away by her parents.

Just how nearly correct my surmises were will be seen further on.

CHAPTER XVII.

I AM constrained to insert the subject matter of this chapter, however much I should prefer to omit it. One cannot expatiate on his own grief. That is not to be expected. It is too sacred to him—too peculiarly his own to be published, yet it seems necessary here, in order to complete, to some extent, the narration of this somewhat kinked chain of happenings.

Toward the close of December, 1892, my mother died. She had not been in good health, as I have before stated, and she contracted a severe cold which developed pneumonia, and being too weak to withstand its vigorous ravages, she fell an easy prey to it. I was left alone. She was my nearest and dearest friend, and the only relative of whom I had any knowledge. My sorrow was keen. I thought if I could but have her back again, I would do anything within my power that would add to her comfort and happiness. I thought, too, of the many, many little deeds that I might have done, that I had left undone. Then it was that I was truly thankful that I could recall many acts and deeds of love that I *had* bestowed upon her; often from a sense of duty, it may be, yet more frequently, I now think, from the promptings of a loving heart. Without these thoughts to console me, I believe that my sorrow would take on an accusative form and would haunt me throughout life.

She was buried by the side of my father in Rose Hill cemetery. There, on that bleak December afternoon, I lingered for a time. "I have two graves now," I soliloquized, "and one is a fresh one. There is room for one more here. There can't be any question as to who will be the next to lie down within this enclosure."

Ah, how we living folks juggle with Death, so to speak! We anticipate him, we measure him, we cut garments to fit him.

It now is my custom to visit this beautiful burial ground frequently. Whatever may be our theories, as to the destiny of the soul, we all have our graves. Of them we are certain. The one who believes in re-incarnation has his, and erects, it may be, a towering shaft of granite thereon. The one whose belief is that the soul

rests within the grave until called by the resur-
rector of the dead, may be seen to train roses
over the tomb.   To him, who thinks that the
soul dies with the body, there comes a silent
prompting to grave upon the slab, a tender
sentiment.   And that one, who inclines to the
belief that immediately after death the soul
wings its way to some realm of bliss, may be
impelled to plant upon his mound of mould, a
shrub of arbor vitæ.   Forgetting for a time our
creeds and isms, we theorists treat our graves
in very much the same manner. We mark them
with stones, variously carved and lettered. We
decorate them with flowers in summer.   They
are charges, in a certain sense, left to our keeping.   Then, too, each one represents a recollection that we would not have put from us, although sorrow be so profoundly blended with it.

Here, by these mounds of mine, I often sit
alone of summer evenings and recall words and
deeds of the departed ones.   It is a sort of
relief, too, to think that the turmoil of life has
not the power to disturb that peaceful rest into
which they have passed, after a comparatively
short participation in the mysterious drama of
life.

On some occasions, when I got furthest away

from myself and deepest into reflection, it occurred to me that then, if ever, was an oppor-
tune time for departed spirits to commune with
the living. I have heard well-remembered
voices and songs, not with my ears, however,
but through my memory. At some times I
have fancied myself under a sort of beneficent
spell that held me as by the influence of a
strangely beautiful unwritten prayer. It is true,
I never was permitted to hear the flutter of
angelic wings, but I have felt the warm tears
start forth, caused by the tacit power of a tender recollection. At such times, however, a
sense of peaceful resignation steals in upon
him, who can, by the faith that is within him,
discern for these silent sleepers, through the
dim vista of the future, the radiance of a glori-
ous resurrection dawn.

CHAPTER XVIII.

I SHALL have to digress far enough to say that at the time I was at Valparaiso, a fashionable wedding took place in a certain Washington boulevard residence, in Chicago. The newspapers had much to say about it at the time. One in particular had written it up in a style, the unique descriptiveness of which must have caused the live-stock editor to turn green with envy. I procured a copy of this same paper and read and reread the article. All the while there was a perceptible fluctuation in the operations of my physical economy,—a congestion somewhere within me that must have caused me to lose color, for my room-mate remarked, "What has happened, Burton? You look as pale as a ghost."

I evaded his question, but it was quite a while before I regained my normal condition, I am sure.

Somewhere, folded away in the bottom of my trunk is that same paper, I have no doubt with blue pencil marks indicating that article. The callow youth is prone to preserve such things, it seems. It is remarkable though, how soon they become "back numbers", so to speak.

It is hardly necessary to explain that the principals in this social event were Miss Florence Gray and Mr. Archie Glynn.

Arthur had been at home a short time, to be present at his sister's marriage, but had gone again before I returned. He was graduated that year, but did not come home until in the winter, so that I had seen but little of him before my mother's death. I remember that on the day of the burial, it was the grasp of his warm hand that brought me back to the realization that I was a temporal being and needed shelter and food.

I was always welcome at Arthur's home, but it was owing to his personality that I felt in the least at ease, for the surroundings were so different from those of the home of our boyhood days.

Now, that my own home was broken up, there was no other place that seemed as much like it as that of kind-hearted, motherly Mrs. Wentworth. There was extended to me a welcome, the sincerity of which could not be equivocated. Then, too, Grace's vivacity was stimulating. I visited them often. Here it was that Arthur found me one Sunday, that winter, and here it was that he and Grace met for the first time for several years. She was in her best mood, and entertained us for a short time, despite the fact that he had called to take me right away with him. After that casual meeting that Sunday afternoon, each of these friends of mine had asked me about the other repeatedly, until I found myself a sort of speaking tube between two souls that had for each other a strong and mutual attraction. I had observed it from the first, and, reading it in the light of the truth as I did, I could but bow to the inevitable.

CHAPTER XIX.

EARLY in March, 1893, I secured a position, through the kindly directed offices of Mr. Wentworth and Judge L—, to do certain work at the World's Fair, for a city newspaper.

A few days before going to take charge of my new duties, however, I went to call on my old friend, Mr. Cay, remembering that I had not seen him for several weeks.

The old man received me with the same exclamation with which he had greeted me for years,—"'Ello Ray, me lad, 'ow do ye do!" And old Trip, now grown quite gray and decrepit, opened his little red mouth and fawned upon me with as beaming a smile as I had ever seen on human face.

How I loved those old-time friends—man and dog!

"I've sold me shop, Ray, and goin' to quit work—gettin' too hold, ye see. The doc says this river'll be the killin' o' me ef I don't git away from 't."

"You are not going away from the city, I
hope, Mr. Cay?" I asked.

"No. I'll be tinkerin'in the shop at 'ome, on
Carroll avenue, ye know."

"I've been lookin' for ye these several days,"
he continued. "'Ere's a small box as was left
'ere by 'Ankins. 'E told me to see that ye got
it, and now I 'ave kept me word with 'im."

I took the parcel, but before quitting his shop,
perhaps for the last time, we had a long chat
about his future arrangements, my prospects,
and some past happenings that took us back to
our first acquaintance. After promising to call
to see him sometimes at his home, I took leave
of him. I went directly to my room so I might
be alone when examining the mysterious box,
left me by one Hankins, whom I had not seen
for many years. As I removed the coarse paper
that was wrapped around the box, I must confess I experienced some queer misgivings. I
thought of all the infernal machines of which I
had ever read, and even gave the dynamite
bomb a serious reflection. These fears were
but momentary, however, and left me when I
remembered that I was no monarch, nor pro-
moter of a trust, nor even a railway president.
No one could have designs on my life, so, with

a steady hand, I proceeded to undo the parcel. I first came to a small pasteboard box, within which was a smaller box of the same material, and inside this one was yet another. You can hardly imagine to what a pitch one's curiosity gets wrought by undoing such a series of concealments, unless you have passed through a like experience. I felt certain that this third box contained the thing itself that Mr. Hankins would have me see, whatever that might be. I opened it carefully, and with my pencil parted some cotton that was on top, and revealed to my astonished eyes, my father's watch. I recognized it at a glance.

I had often dreamed that father had come back to live with us again, and that same feeling of glad surprise which I experienced on seeing him, in my dreams, was now partly realized on beholding once more his watch, which I never expected to see again. My earliest recollection of it was when he used to place it against my ear, and sometimes allowed me to hold it in my hands. I wept and laughed by turns, like any girl.

In the bottom of the box was a piece of writing paper, folded rather clumsily, which I opened and read. The composition bore marks of laborious effort in every particular. It was written by Mr. Hankins and addressed to me personally. He explained that he had received the watch from two sailors, and recognized it by my father's initials on the inside of the case.

They confessed to having taken it and a small sum of money from my father, but protested that they had not thrown him into the river. They said that he had fallen in, when trying to free himself from their grasp.

He further explained that this took place on an out voyage in the upper lake region and that after they landed at Duluth he never saw anything more of these men.

In my own mind, I concluded that Hankins had been an accomplice in this dastardly crime. He probably knew of my father's plans and saw him get the money at the bank. The more I thought of it, the more firm I grew in my opinion that he was connected with it. I resolved to do some sleuthing on my own account. I kept the matter of the watch a secret, but told Mr. Cay to be sure to tell Hankins that I wished to see him, if he chanced to call on him again.

But after all, why a robber should return an old watch, the intrinsic value of which could not exceed ten dollars, after so many years, was more than I could understand.

I prized the old time-piece highly, notwithstanding that the return of it caused me to suspect the man who had taken the trouble to return it to me.

CHAPTER XX.

I HAD rented the old cottage on Morgan street to a small family soon after my mother's death, and Miss Baldwin, my kind-hearted teacher, had gone to live with friends on the North Side. I had been to see her just before I began work in Jackson park, at which time she told me that she intended spending a large portion of her time at the World's Fair during the summer, after which she thought she would return to her New England home.

She owned two vacant lots on the north shore, that she had bought some years before as an investment, she said, and was now quite elated over the fact that they had appreciated considerably of late, largely because they had appended to them that mysterious yet highly valuable something that obtains only on abutting property, styled "riparian rights." And that reminds anyone who may take the trouble to look into the matter, that there is not much ˙ said about those same rights by real estate

people on the South Side,—probably because
the larger portion of them was gathered in by
a certain incorporation, (whose porcine pro-
clivities it is pretty generally conceded are
abnormally large,) long before there was
much value attached to them on the outlying
north shore.

It was a source of much satisfaction to me
that Miss Baldwin's investment had proved to
be a good one, for she was so industrious and
deserving that it seemed to me that there could
come to her no fortune so good but that she
would fully merit it. She displayed good judgment, too, in disposing of her lots that spring,
since the depreciation that set in that fall has
hardly yet reached the bottom of the scale.

About this time it was that I called one day
at the store of E. L. Warp & Co., to greet my
old associates, and Frank in particular.

Poor boy, I felt sorry for him! He was working on, just where he began, with no prospects
in sight for anything better. True, his salary
had been increased a time or two, yet there
seemed to be no place open to him for advancement. Mr. Hildebrand had taken a sort of dis-
like to him, too, despite his honesty and faith-
fulness. His antipathy partook somewhat of

that same spirit that sometimes leads a man to step out of his way to kick a faithful, yet fawning dog.

I made up my mind to try to find something better for Frank, and by securing the co-operation of some of my friends, we were enabled to place him as shipping clerk in a wholesale furnishing goods house, where he is to-day, a valuable and trusted employe.

Arthur had taken the law course in the University of Michigan, and had now set up as a lawyer. He was associated with an old friend of his father, who had an extensive practice. His prospects, therefore, were somewhat better than those of the average beginner.

At this time Arthur was a frequent caller at the home of the Wentworths. Grace was highly pleased, I was sure, because she had asked me questions about him and his prospects in the most innocent way possible. I was the older brother, you see, and she treated me as such. Never did I allow this artless little sister to know that any other kind of love had ever found lodgment in my heart. Mrs. Wentworth was just too tickled to conceal the fact,—but that was quite motherly and natural, for Arthur was good, manly, rather prepossessing in appearance, and back of all that was the fact that his father was a weal*h*y man. Mr. Wentworth, I believe, was rather passive on the subject, but of course he could raise no objections. Arthur had interrogated me, too, quite as artlessly as had Grace. There seemed to be open to me a remarkable opportunity—a double role of "Brother."

CHAPTER XXI.

"ELYSIAN FIELDS" would have been a good name for Jackson Park during the summer of 1893. "White City" was very appropriate, "Dream City" was much written of, but "World's Fair" was the everyday name by which it was called, notwithstanding the fact that officially it was the "World's Columbian Exposition."

Here it was that I put in six or seven months of steady work that came more nearly to being amusement than anything that I had ever done. Not because my work was light, certainly, but on account of the surroundings. I think this was pretty generally the case with all classes of workers on the grounds. A position here was looked upon as an opportunity and not as a task. Why, I was told that among the sweepers in the Illinois building was an ex-congressman. If that were the case I am confident that he never has had occasion to regret the fact that he accepted, for a time, so humble a position. He is none the less respected to-day because he worked out his tuition in that greatest of universities.

That Columbian guard whom I knew only as "Cap," doubtless has finished his college course, and may now occupy an enviable position in life. I have no doubt however, that when he looks back over his past life for "red letter" days, he finds that many of them occurred in the summer of 1893.

Among my chair-pusher acquaintances was one young man in whom I became much interested. He was so intelligent and well-bred that one could not help liking him. He was not a college student. Most likely he had a better knowledge of Jersey cattle and Clydesdale horses than he had of Latin roots and logarithms. It was his ambition, however, to prepare to enter the University of Chicago and sometime to be graduated from it. Whether he followed up that plan and is now a student in that institution that borders on the once famous Midway, or was led by circumstances along some other path of duty, in his country home, I shall always think that he found those days spent at the "push" end of a chair an excellent preparative.

In this delightful place one never grew tired of the scenes about him. The eye could follow those beautiful perspectives that displayed facades of magnificent architecture, greenwood isles, and sparkling lagoons, and in a short time review them with renewed interest. The one who feasted much on these outdoor scenes and afterward traveled abroad, marveled little, it seems to me, on beholding for the first time the streets of Venice or the celebrated Champs Elysees,—nor did he manifest much surprise at the magnitude of the Coliseum.

Volumes might be written in a reminiscent way by any one who spent much time at that great exposition, as, indeed, much has been published aside from official statistics; but I must beg pardon for this slight digression, and pass on to that part that relates to the tale.

One of my evening duties was to report casualties from a certain number of emergency hospitals, as well as from the regular ones· There was one day, I remember, that they were taxed beyond their several capacities. With the imaginings of an old schoolmaster, I see, in my mind, a hundred hands go up, displaying their owners' eagerness to explain that my meaning is anticipated.   Yes, it was the 9th of October—"Chicago Day," if you so prefer it.

When one stops to think of it, there certainly are many people in this big world who have a vivid recollection of that particular day and its throng.

I had but started on my round that evening when I noticed the men lifting a patient from an ambulance at one of the hospitals, who looked familiar.   I stepped nearer and saw that it was Mr. Wentworth, very pale and apparently dead.   He had been caught in the jam at the terminal station and trampled upon and otherwise seriously injured, the wagon attendant explained.   I sent a messenger to the office for a relief; and, being acquainted with the head attendant at the hospital, was permitted to remain near Mr. Wentworth, and finally to assist in caring for him, as there was a dearth of nurses.   I had not long to watch, however. Once, just before the physician got around to his cot, he opened his eyes and fastened them upon me.   There was in them a look of anguish that cannot be described.   He seemed to recognize me and made an effort to speak, but no sound could he utter.   He squeezed my hand for an instant, then relaxed his hold, closed his eyes and relapsed into a sort of comatose condition, from which the physician was unable to arouse him. He was dead. It thus became my painful duty to convey to Mrs. Wentworth news as sad as was that which she once brought to our home on Morgan street. Permit me to draw the curtain here.

CHAPTER XXII.

TWO years have passed since Mr. Wentworth's death, and it is again October. Time has wrought its usual number of changes, although the economy of nature goes on, undisturbed by the hopes and fears, the joys and sorrows of men.

Archie Glynn's father had failed financially soon after the marriage of that fastidious young man, which threw him upon his own resources—or his father-in-law. Having some of the American grit mixed with his affected make-up, he got down to real work, developing the former, to the everlasting detriment of the latter. By making what he could of his somewhat neglected law business, and teaching for several months in the night schools, he succeeded in getting upon his feet, so to speak, by the end of the first year after the disaster, and is now doing fairly well, Arthur tells me.

Arthur and Grace were married a year ago, in a very quiet manner. They are a congenial couple in the strictest sense, and it would be a hard matter to find a happier pair anywhere. I enjoy a brother's privileges in their home, which is no small consideration to a man whose home is where he takes off his hat—allowing this to be descriptive of one's standing in a boarding house or hotel.

Among Mr. Wentworth's papers in his strong box, was a sealed envelope addressed to me, and which was delivered to me soon after his decease. The contents has been kept a profound secret by me until now. Omitting the date and address, it read thus:

"Doubtless you are aware of the fact that it has been my wish that my daughter, Grace, and you should marry. If this desired wish should ever be realized, will you not, for her sake, keep the contents of this letter forever a secret? Should your marriage with her never take place, however, then it is my wish that you use this letter as a voucher in securing an equitable adjustment of matters hereinafter explained, in which my wife and daughter will co-operate, when they come to know the facts.

You probably remember some of the circumstances connected with your father's death. He drew four thousand dollars from the bank in the afternoon, and came to my place about four o'clock. There he found a telegram awaiting him which informed him that the man with whom he was about to close a deal would be away from home for a few days and that he should come on a stated date later. After reading the message he went away to attend to some business, but returned again later in the evening, at which time he expressed a wish to leave his wallet in my safe, as the banks were closed. On leaving he went out at the back door, as he had often done before. I closed it after him and immediately locked up for the night. The next morning I went to the store earlier than usual, and saw some men dragging the river near the bridge. They soon hauled a body ashore which proved to be your father. I was so thoroughly excited that I did not think of the wallet until late that day. Then it was that the tempter said 'Let it remain in its hiding. The supposition is that it was taken by the robbers.' I was weak enough to delay, and each day that I procrastinated made an explanation all the more difficult, until I gave up in despair. There was but one person who suspected me, and that one is now dead.

I have led a miserable life ever since. I have suffered much and I have deserved to suffer much. I beg your forgiveness."

After reading this letter, and reflecting on

the rigid economy that my mother was compelled to practice after father's death, I literally gnashed my teeth and tore my hair.

This man would have me marry his daughter so that his family should never know what a rascal he really was, and, at the same time, square matters to a certain extent with his conscience.

I meditated upon this letter for many days. That four thousand dollars was mine by right, to say nothing of interest. Here arose a difficulty, however, that was not easily bridged. These were my nearest friends and how could I apprise them of this obligation without ruthlessly throwing open the door of their family closet and revealing the grewsome, grinning skeleton therein concealed?

I, too, procrastinated.

This, secret, however, has become burdensome to me. I have longed to tell it to some one, and thus relieve my mind; so, my patient reader, I have told the facts to you in a tale, a stray copy of which I earnestly hope may never fall into the hands of these dear friends of mine.

THE END.